'Twas the Night Before Christmas

GROSSET & DUNLAP
Published by the Penguin Group
Penguin Group (USA) Inc., 375 Hudson Street, New York, New York 10014, USA
Penguin Group (Canada), 90 Eglinton Avenue East, Suite 700,
Toronto, Ontario M4P 2Y3, Canada
(a division of Pearson Penguin Canada Inc.)
Penguin Books Ltd., 80 Strand, London WC2R 0RL, England
Penguin Group Ireland, 25 St. Stephen's Green, Dublin 2, Ireland
(a division of Penguin Books Ltd.)
Penguin Group (Australia), 250 Camberwell Road, Camberwell, Victoria 3124, Australia
(a division of Pearson Australia Group Pty. Ltd.)
Penguin Books India Pvt. Ltd., 11 Community Centre, Panchsheel Park,
New Delhi—110 017, India
Penguin Group (NZ), 67 Apollo Drive, Rosedale, North Shore 0632, New Zealand
(a division of Pearson New Zealand Ltd.)
Penguin Books (South Africa) (Pty.) Ltd., 24 Sturdee Avenue,
Rosebank, Johannesburg 2196, South Africa

Penguin Books Ltd., Registered Offices:
80 Strand, London WC2R 0RL, England

Library of Congress Control Number: 2008010690

ISBN 978-0-448-44975-3   10 9 8 7 6 5 4 3 2 1

'Twas the Night Before Christmas

By Ellie O'Ryan

Illustrated by John and Tonja Huxtable

Based on the television series *Super WHY!*,
created by Angela C. Santomero, as seen on PBS KIDS

Grosset & Dunlap

It was Christmas Eve in Storybrook Village. That's where Whyatt Beanstalk and all his fairy-tale friends lived.

All the houses in the village were decorated with twinkling lights that shimmered in the evening light. Whyatt shivered with excitement as he walked home. After all, Christmas at the Beanstalk house was a very special time!

"It's the night before Christmas," began Whyatt, "and all through the house—"

"Not a creature was stirring—not even Baby Joy," continued Whyatt's mother. "And you know who will be coming soon?"

"Santa Claus!" Whyatt yelled as he jumped up and down.

"*Shhh*," Whyatt's mom whispered. "You'll wake Baby Joy. But you're right. Tonight Santa's going to visit you and all the other children."

As Whyatt's mother left to put Joy in her crib, Whyatt wondered, "Why does Santa visit on Christmas?"

As Whyatt tried to think of the answer he paced back and forth. "That's a super-big question . . . and a super-big question needs us, the Super Readers!"

Whyatt raced to the Book Club where he met the other Super Readers: Pig, Red Riding Hood, and Princess Pea.

"Okay, Whyatt, ask your question," said Red Riding Hood.

"I want to know *why* Santa visits on Christmas," replied Whyatt.

"What a wonderrific question!" Red Riding Hood said with a grin.

"And when we have a question, we look in a book!" Whyatt finished.

"Which book should we look in?" asked Pig.

Princess Pea waved her wand and sparkles swirled in the air. "Peas and carrots, carrots and peas. Book come out, please, please, please!" she chanted.

A book twirled and whirled from the tippy-top of the bookshelves and floated down to the Super Readers. The title was *'Twas the Night Before Christmas*.

'Twas the Night
Before Christmas

"We need to transform into super heroes and jump into this book!" said Whyatt. "If we can find all the red, sparkly SUPER LETTERS hidden in this story, we will be able to answer my question. Now it's time to transform!"

Alpha Pig with Alphabet Power!

WONDER RED WITH WORD POWER!

Princess Presto with Spelling Power!

Super Why with the Power to Read!

The Super Readers jumped into their Why Flyers, strapped on their helmets, and buckled their seat belts. Then they flew into *'Twas the Night Before Christmas*. "Super Readers . . . to the rescue!" they called as they zoomed off in their Why Flyers.

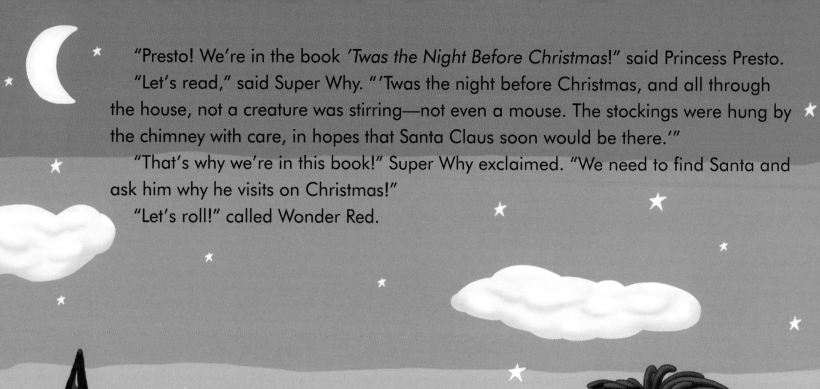

"Presto! We're in the book *'Twas the Night Before Christmas!*" said Princess Presto.

"Let's read," said Super Why. "'Twas the night before Christmas, and all through the house, not a creature was stirring—not even a mouse. The stockings were hung by the chimney with care, in hopes that Santa Claus soon would be there.'"

"That's why we're in this book!" Super Why exclaimed. "We need to find Santa and ask him why he visits on Christmas!"

"Let's roll!" called Wonder Red.

Night began to fall as the Super Readers walked through a small village. Suddenly, Super Why pointed to the star-filled sky. "There's Santa! And he's got a sleigh full of toys," said Super Why. "But look! Some of the toys are falling out of Santa's sack! We have to help him. But how?"

13

"Alpha Pig . . . to the rescue! With my Amazing Alphabet Tools, I can catch Santa's toys!" Alpha Pig exclaimed. He ran beneath the sleigh with his Alphabet-net. "Here comes a toy! Quick! Let's catch it!"

He raced under a stuffed elephant and caught it just in time. "What's this letter?" he asked, pointing to a tag on the toy's neck. "It's an E—for ELEPHANT! And here come two more toys!" he called, swinging his net. "Got them! This one has a K—for KITE! And this one has a Z—for ZEBRA!"

"Lickety letters! We caught all of Santa's toys!" said Alpha Pig. "Let's give ourselves a big thumbs-up."

"Super duper!" Super Why cheered. "Now let's find Santa."

The Super Readers raced through the snow and found Santa sitting in his sleigh in front of a house.

"Ho, ho, ho, Super Readers! What a nice surprise!" said Santa.

"Here you go, Santa," said Alpha Pig. "You dropped these toys."

"Thanks, Super Readers! I better get going. I have lots of presents to deliver," said Santa as he grabbed the sleigh reins. "Now, on Prancer! On Donner! On Blitzen!"

"Santa, wait!" Super Why cried. "I have a question for you!" As Santa's
sleigh flew high into the night sky, two sparkly Super Letters fell to the ground.
"Don't worry, Super Why," said Princess Presto. "We'll catch up with Santa."
"To Santa!" Wonder Red exclaimed.

As the Super Readers sped through the snowy village, Wonder Red gasped, "Look! Santa's sleigh is up on the roof of that house! But where's Santa?"

Just then, a wide-eyed little boy opened the door. "Santa?" he asked as he looked around.

"No, we're the Super Readers," Super Why said. "And who are you?"

"I'm Alex," answered the boy.

"We're looking for Santa. Is he in your house?" Super Why asked hopefully.

"No," replied Alex sadly. "I can't find him anywhere. How can we get Santa to come to my house?"

"Cue the sparkles, cue the music—Princess Presto . . . to the rescue! With my Magic Spelling Wand, I can spell the word SNACK," Princess Presto said. "Santa loves snacks! It says so in all of the Santa stories. Maybe a snack will bring Santa here."

Princess Presto raised her wand and said, "S-N-A-C-K. That spells SNACK! Presto!" In a burst of sparkles, a tall glass of milk and a plate of cookies appeared.

"Spectacular spelling!" cried Princess Presto. "We made a snack for Santa. And look, another Super Letter!"

Just then, the Super Readers heard a sound coming from outside. They rushed out the door.

Could it really be Santa?

Just as the Super Readers hoped, they saw Santa standing on the roof.

"Ho! Ho! Ho! Merry Christmas!" Santa said.

"Santa! It's you!" Super Why cheered. "Come inside!"

"I can't," Santa said sadly. "There's no chimney on this house, and I *always* come down the chimney. Even my story says so, see?"

Santa Claus comes down the chimney.

"Super Why . . . to the rescue! With the Power to Read, I can change this story and save the day!" Super Why said. "Let's change the word CHIMNEY."

Zzzap! Super Why used his Why Writer to zap the word CHIMNEY out of the sentence.

"Now, which word will help Santa get down and into the house—RIVER, LADDER, or SHOE?" asked Super Why. "Let's try RIVER! Ready, set, zzzap!"

Super Why zapped RIVER into the sentence and read it again. "Santa Claus comes down the RIVER."

Right before their eyes, Santa came whooshing down a river on a raft!

"Down the river I go! Ho, ho, whoahhh!" laughed Santa.

river
ladder
shoe

Santa Claus comes down the river.

river
ladder
shoe

Santa Claus comes down the ladder.

"That didn't help Santa get into the house. Let's try the word LADDER instead! Ready, set, *zzzap!*" said Super Why. He zapped the word LADDER into the sentence with his Why Writer. "Santa Claus comes down the LADDER," read Super Why.

Zzzap! A candy-cane ladder appeared. Santa climbed down it and went inside the house!

"Super job, Super Readers," said Super Why. "We changed the story and helped Santa get into the house!"

The Super Readers went back inside the house and found Santa standing in Alex's living room.

"Ho, ho, ho, everyone! All this work has made me hungry. Thanks for the snack," said Santa as he took a bite of cookie and a sip of milk. "So, Super Readers. What brings you into my story on Christmas Eve?"

"We have a question for you," Super Why said. "Why do you always visit on Christmas?"

"That's a good question!" replied Santa. "When I was a little boy, I made presents and gave them to my family. I loved how happy it made them. And it made me happy, too."

"Wow, Santa!" said Super Why.

"Maybe I can do something to make my brothers happy on Christmas," Alpha Pig exclaimed. "I can make them a race car!"

"I can make up a song for my family—and sing it to them!" said Princess Presto.

"I can make Grandma's favorite cookies," added Wonder Red.

"Maybe I can make something for my family, too," Super Why said.

"Great ideas, Super Readers," said Santa. Then he turned to Alex and handed him a present. "Oh! I almost forgot. Merry Christmas!"

"A present? For me?" Alex gasped.

"I made it myself," Santa said proudly.

"Gee, thanks, Santa!" said Alex.

"Say, Super Readers. How about a ride on my sleigh before you go home?" asked Santa.

The Super Readers cheered as they went outside and climbed into Santa's sleigh.
"Well, ho, ho, ho. Let's go, go, gooooooo!" said Santa as they lifted into the air.
As they soared across the starry night sky, the Super Readers sang, "Jingle bells, jingle
bells, jingle all the way. Oh what fun it is to read, the Super Readers saved the day!"

After their magical Christmas Eve sleigh ride, the Super Readers landed safely back on the ground. They also found the last two Super Letters.

"We've got all our Super Letters!" Super Why exclaimed. "Now we can go back to the Book Club and answer my question."

"Thanks for the ride, Santa!" said the Super Readers. "Merry Christmas! Good-bye, Alex! Good-bye, Santa!"

"Why Flyers, back to the Book Club!" said Super Why as the Super Readers jumped into their Why Flyers and zoomed back to the Book Club.

At the Book Club, the Super Readers transformed back into their storybook selves.

With a *whiz* and a *zzzap*, Whyatt made all the Super Letters appear on the Super-Duper Computer.

"H-A-P-P-Y. Our Super Letters spell HAPPY," Whyatt said. "But why?"

Then he thought about everything they'd learned from Santa. "Santa visits children because it makes them happy—and it makes him happy, too! That's the answer to my question!"

Whyatt hurried home from the Book Club. After all, it was almost bedtime and Santa would be visiting his house very soon! But there was one very important thing that Whyatt had to do first. He gathered up colored paper, markers, crayons, scissors, and glue, and got to work on a very special present for his family.

The next morning, Whyatt and his family woke up early. "Merry Christmas, everybody!" Whyatt said. "I made something for all of you. It's a book about our whole family. I wrote the words and drew the pictures!"

"Thank you, Whyatt," said his father. "It's wonderful. And it's even more wonderful that you made it yourself. It makes us so happy."

"You're welcome," Whyatt said with a grin. "It makes me happy, too!"

Jingle bells, jingle bells, jingle all the way.
Calling friends in Storybrook for a super holiday.
Jingle bells, jingle bells, jingle all the way.
Oh what fun it is to read, the Super Readers saved the day.
Jingle bells, jingle bells, jingle all the way.
We're all here to spread some cheer, hip, hip, holiday hurray!